Beauty and the Beast

Level 3

Retold by Fiona Kalinowski
Series Editor: Melanie Williams

Pearson Education Limited
Pearson
KAO Two
KAO Park
Harlow
Essex
CM17 9NA

and Associated Companies throughout the world.

ISBN 9781292240060

First published by Librairie du Liban Publishers, 1996
This adaptation first published by
Penguin Books 2000
1 3 5 7 9 10 8 6 4 2

Text copyright © Pearson Education Limited 2000
Illustrations copyright ©1996 Librairie du Liban

Retold by Fiona Kalinowski
Series Editor: Melanie Williams
Designed by Shireen Nathoo Design
Illustrated by Kay Dixey

Printed in Brazil by Docuprint DCPT 220206

The moral right of the author and illustrator have been asserted

All rights reserved; no part of this publication may be reproduced, stored in a retrieval system, or transmitted in any form or by any means, electronic, mechanical, photocopying, recording, or otherwise, without the prior written permission of the Publishers.

Published by Pearson Education Limited

For a complete list of titles available in the Pearson Story Readers series please write to your local Pearson Education office or contact:
Pearson, KAO Two, KAO Park, Harlow, Essex, CM17 9NA

Answers for the Activities in this book are published in the free Pearson English Story Readers Factsheet on the website, www.pearsonenglishreaders.com

Once upon a time, a long time ago, a rich man lived with his family in a big house in a town beside the sea. He loved his family, but his favorite child was his youngest daughter, Beauty. She was kind and beautiful, like her mother, who died when the children were young.

The man was a merchant. Every week, his ships arrived from countries far away, full of interesting things. These he sold at the market in the town.

One winter, there was a terrible storm and all his ships were lost at sea. The family got poorer and poorer and had to move to a smaller house. With the little money he had, the merchant decided to buy a small farm in the country.

All the family had to work very hard on the farm. Every day, they had to milk the cows, give the hens food, work in the fields, and cut wood for the fire. At the end of every day, they were tired.

"Oh, I wish we were back in our big house," said the sisters.

"I wish we could watch the ships come and go again," said the brothers.

Only Beauty was happy. She enjoyed working with her father.

After some months on the farm, Beauty's father decided to go visit friends in town and to buy some things the family needed for the farm.

"I'll be away all day," he told his children. "Be good while I'm away. Remember to milk the cows and give the hens their food."

Then he got on his horse, waved to his children, waved again to Beauty, and rode to town.

In the afternoon, it started to get cold. By the evening, when he was riding home, it was very cold and windy.

"Oh dear, I'm not going to get home tonight," thought the merchant. "I need to find somewhere to stay the night. It's too cold to stay outside."

It was very late at night when he saw a big house in front of him. The house was lit up inside and it looked warm and welcoming. "Perhaps I can stay here for the night," thought the merchant. "I do hope so."

He rode up to the house and then found a place for his horse behind it. Next he walked quickly to the front and knocked on the door. No one came. He knocked again. No one came, but the door opened slowly.

The merchant looked in. He saw a very big room with a big table in the middle and candles on the table. There was food on the table. A big fire was burning in the fireplace.

The merchant was cold and hungry, and he wanted to stand in front of the fire and eat some of the food. He knocked on the door again, but again there was no answer.

"Hello," he cried loudly. "Is anyone here?"

No one answered.

Slowly, the merchant walked into the room. He looked all around. No one was there.

"Hello," he cried again. "Is anyone at home?" But again, there was no answer.

"This is strange," he thought, "but the food smells good and I'm so hungry!"

He took off his coat and sat at the table. "I'll eat just a little," he thought.

He ate a little, then a little more, then he ate all of it. It tasted so good.

That night the merchant slept in one of the many bedrooms in the house. The bed was soft and warm, and he slept all night. In the morning, when he woke up, his old clothes were not there. In their place he saw a beautiful new blue suit, a white shirt, and new gray shoes. He put them on and looked at himself in the mirror. "Very nice. Very handsome!" He smiled at himself in the mirror.

It was a beautiful day and the merchant went out into the garden.

"What a strange place this is," he thought. "It's fall, but this garden is full of flowers. I haven't seen anyone, but there were these new clothes in the bedroom this morning. And yesterday, there was hot food on the table. Very strange! I'll just take some roses for Beauty and then go."

As soon as he took a rose, there was a terrible cry from behind him. The merchant turned around quickly. He could not believe his eyes! There in front of him stood an ugly monster.
He was half man and half beast, with an ugly face and hands like an animal. He had on beautiful clothes.

"I gave you food, and I gave you clothes. Why are you taking my beautiful roses?" the Beast cried.

"They're for Beauty, my youngest daughter," the merchant whispered. He was very scared.

" Ah, yes," said the Beast, "I've seen your beautiful daughter in my magic mirror. I know. Bring your beautiful daughter for my beautiful roses. If you don't, you and your family will die."

The merchant rode home. Every time he thought of Beauty, he started to cry. Every time he thought of the Beast, he was afraid.

"Oh, what am I going to do?" he asked himself again and again.

When he arrived home, he started to cry again. Slowly, he told his family about his night in the strange house and about the ugly beast.

"We'll all die if Beauty doesn't go to him. I don't know what to do!"

"Father," said Beauty. "I'll go to him. I'm scared, it's true, but I have to go. I don't want everyone to die. Let's go now."

So they rode back to the Beast's house that same day.

When they arrived at the big house, the Beast was waiting for them.

"Good evening, Beauty," he said quietly.

Poor Beauty could not speak. She was too scared.

The Beast turned to her father. "You may stay for one night," he said.

"Then tomorrow you must go home."

That night Beauty did not sleep well. She thought about her brothers and sisters. She thought about her father. She thought about the farm and all the animals on the farm. In the end, she cried herself to sleep.

In the morning, when she woke up, her old clothes were not there. In their place she saw a lovely dress with a black, red, and white hat to match. She put them on and then went to say goodbye to her father.

Later that morning, she walked through the house and looked in all the rooms. Soon, she came to a room with her name on the door. She went in. It was a lovely room. There were roses from the garden on the table, and Beauty started to feel a little happier.

Then she saw a mirror on the wall. In the mirror, she could see her brothers and her father! Her father was on his horse, and he was arriving back home. He looked very sad. Beauty started to cry again.

Just then, the Beast came into the room.

"Come into the garden," he said, "and sit beside the roses. They'll make you feel happier."

In the garden, the Beast gave Beauty a rose.

"The mirror in your room is magic," he explained. "When you look into the mirror, you'll always see your family. Then you'll not need to be so sad."

Every day after that, Beauty looked in the mirror and saw her family working in the fields or in the house. Every day, she was a little happier.

In the evening, she always had dinner with the Beast. She talked about her family. Her brothers and sisters worked hard. They wanted to live in a beautiful house like her. "But I want to be with them, wherever they are!" she said. The Beast was kind and listened to her.

One day, in the mirror, Beauty saw her father in bed. He was very sick.

"I...I must go home to see my father," she said to the Beast. "He's very sick. Please let me go. I'll come back as soon as he is better."

"You may go," said the Beast. "But take my ring with you. Look at it every day. If it turns dark, you'll know that I am sick and you must come back."

Beauty went to see her father. He was very happy to see her, and he soon began to get well again. They talked about the Beast. Beauty told her father she used to cry a lot. "But now I like him. Every day I like him a little more."

Her father said, "He looks so strange and frightening and I want you here with me."

"But he's kind and friendly," Beauty answered simply.

When her father was better, they went for short walks around the farm. Beauty liked being with her father, but she often thought about the Beast too. Every day, she looked at his ring to make sure that he was not sick.

Then one day, the ring was dark!

"Father, I must go. My friend is sick, and I must go help him."

She rode back to the Beast's house as quickly as she could. When she arrived, she found him in the garden. He was lying beside the roses, one rose in his hand. His face was white and he looked very sick.

"Oh, my dear friend, you mustn't die," cried Beauty. She kissed his white face.

As soon as she kissed him, there was a noise like thunder and a brilliant light. Beauty quickly closed her eyes. When she opened them again, a handsome young prince stood in front of her.

"Thank you, Beauty," he said. "Your kiss has broken the magic spell that my uncle made many years ago. He made me into a beast so that he could be king. I needed the kiss of a beautiful woman to break his terrible spell."

Beauty and the prince were very happy together and they were soon married.

A few months later, the prince was king of his country and Beauty was his queen. They lived happily ever after.

ACTIVITIES

BEFORE YOU READ

1. **Look at the pictures on the cover of the book.**
   a. Who are these two people?
   b. Where are they?
   c. Why do you think she is crying?

2. **Look at the pictures on page 3.**
   a. Who do you think these people are?
   b. Who is the man?
   c. Who is the girl with the flower in her hand?
   d. Where does the family live?
   e. Are they rich or poor?

3. **Now look at the picture on page 5.**
   a. Where is the family now?
   b. What do you think has happened?
   c. Do you think this is a sad story?
   d. What do you think happens at the end?

4. **On page 22, Beauty is looking into a mirror.**
   Can you make a sentence with the words below that describes what Beauty could see?

two	*could*	*she*	*father*
her	*and*	*see*	*brothers*

AFTER YOU READ

1. **Mirror writing**
   Have you looked at a word in a mirror? It looks different!
   Write your name on a paper, then look at it in a mirror. Try to write what you see.

   Now try to write: beauty, prince, king, queen

2. **With a partner, put these words in alphabetical order. See who can do it fastest! Here is the alphabet to help you.**

   a b c d e f g h i j k l m n o p q r s t u v w x y z

opened	waved	cried	saw
arrived	put	gave	rode
whispered	thought	explained	lived
decide	date	took	needed

3. **Look at each sentence.**
   Who said this? When? Where were they?
   a. "What a strange place this is."
   b. "I'm scared, it's true, but I have to go."
   c. "Take my ring with you."